Family Story Collection

Always Keep an Open Mind

STORIES ABOUT FAIRNESS AND GOOD JUDGMENT

Book Five

Book Five

Always Keep
an Open Mind

Stories About Fairness and Good Judgment

Introduction

Keeping an open mind about new situations, different people, and unusual experiences can be frightening to a child because these things are unfamiliar. Many children close themselves off from new experiences in order to feel safe. But when they branch out and try new things, a whole world of opportunity opens before them.

Roger and Anita, in "Puppies, Puppies, Everywhere!" think fifteen dogs are a lot to handle, but when faced with one hundred and one dogs, they don't hesitate for a second. Their decision enriches their lives and the lives of those around them. In "Home Is Where the Heart Is," O'Malley distrusts humans, but when he sweeps aside his preconceived ideas and opens his mind, he learns that things aren't always as they seem—sometimes they are even better.

Puppies, Puppies, Everywhere!

from *101 Dalmatians*

***

The more, the merrier!

Pongo and Perdy, along with ninety-nine Dalmatian pups, were on their way home. They were still covered in the soot they had used to disguise themselves so they could escape from Cruella De Vil, who had dognapped the puppies because she wanted to make a coat out of their fur!

Meanwhile, Roger and Anita tried to make the best of Christmas without their beloved dogs. "I can't believe that Pongo and Perdy would run away," Roger said sadly.

"Sometimes at night I can hear them barking," the housekeeper, Nanny, said. "But it always turns out I'm dreaming."

Just then, Nanny, Roger, and Anita *did* hear barking . . . coming from outside. Nanny threw open the front door as Pongo and Perdy bounded into the house with the puppies in tow.

Roger took out a handkerchief and wiped the soot from Pongo's face. "Pongo, boy, is that you?" he exclaimed with delight.

Anita wiped Perdy's face with her

apron. "And Perdy, my darling!" she cried.

Then Nanny proceeded to dust off Pongo and Perdy's puppies. There was Patch, Rolly, Penny, Freckles, little Lucky, and all the others.

"And look!" Nanny cried, scanning the room. "There are more!"

Anita could hardly believe her eyes.

"There must be a hundred of them!" she cried.

Together, Roger, Anita, and Nanny started counting. There were thirty-six pups on the stairs, eleven on the chair, eighteen on the window seat, six behind the couch, and thirteen more being dusted off by Nanny.

"Let's see now," Roger said, doing the math. "That's eighty-four." He added Pongo and Perdy and their fifteen pups, which brought the grand total to . . .

"One hundred and one!" Anita exclaimed.

Where did they come from? And what would Roger and Anita do with them all?

Roger and Anita had already had a lot to handle with Pongo, Perdy, and all their puppies. Did they have room in their lives for one hundred and one Dalmatians?

But Roger did not hesitate for a moment. "We'll keep 'em!" he declared. "We'll buy a big place in the country!"

The dogs barked in agreement. Roger and Anita hugged. Then Roger tiptoed his way through the puppy-filled room and sat down at the piano. He began to sing a song about their new life out in the country, in a home made all the more happy and loving by their new family members—all eighty-four of them!

Home Is Where the Heart Is

from *The Aristocats*

Don't knock it till you've tried it.

I t was time for Duchess and O'Malley to go their separate ways, but they could not find the right words to say good-bye.

"I don't know what to say," Duchess confessed. She and O'Malley were very different. She was an aristocat who lived in a Paris mansion with her adoring owner, Madame Bonfamille. O'Malley was an alley cat from the countryside. But in the short time since they had met, the two cats had become dear friends.

O'Malley had helped Duchess and her three kittens find their way home after Madame's evil butler, Edgar, had abandoned them outside the city. Now, at last, the cats were home. The kittens ran to the door while Duchess and O'Malley said their good-byes.

"Maybe just a short, sweet good-bye would be easiest," O'Malley suggested.

Duchess wished that O'Malley would stay. But O'Malley did not trust humans. He did not believe that they truly cared about their pets. Sadly, Duchess turned to go inside.

"Well, I guess they won't need me anymore," O'Malley said as he watched the door close behind

Duchess and the kittens.

Little did O'Malley know how much the cats really needed him—and at that very

moment! Seconds after they walked through the door, Edgar trapped them in a large sack. He was determined to get rid of them for good. Once they were out of the way, Edgar would become the sole heir to Madame's estate.

Luckily, Roquefort the mouse saw what

had happened and ran after O'Malley.

"Duchess . . . kittens . . . in trouble!" Roquefort managed to say, all out of breath. "Butler did it."

O'Malley sprang into action. He sent Roquefort to get help from O'Malley's alley-cat friends while he raced to Madame's house. He arrived in time to see Edgar carrying the sack of cats into the barn. There the butler locked them inside a steamer trunk. He was going to ship Duchess and the kittens all the way to Timbuktu!

"And this time, you'll never come back!" Edgar said with a nasty chuckle.

But O'Malley had other ideas. He jumped on Edgar, knocking him over. Edgar stumbled, grabbed a pitchfork, and chased after O'Malley. Then Roquefort arrived with

Scat Cat and the other alley cats.

They cornered Edgar while Roquefort freed Duchess and the kittens from the trunk.

Then, working together, the alley cats made Edgar back up toward Frou Frou the horse, who kicked the butler across the barn and into the trunk. The lid slammed shut. Soon, a truck arrived to pick up the trunk, and Edgar was on *his* way to Timbuktu!

When Madame discovered that Duchess and the kittens were back, she was so relieved that she asked O'Malley to stay. "We need a man around the house," she said with a smile.

After nearly losing Duchess and the kittens, O'Malley couldn't bear to leave them again. And once he met Madame, O'Malley realized he had been wrong about humans. Not only did Madame welcome O'Malley, she also took in all his alley-cat friends. If that wasn't caring, O'Malley didn't know what was.

Oh, and living in a mansion wasn't all bad, either!